The Witch's Children Go to School

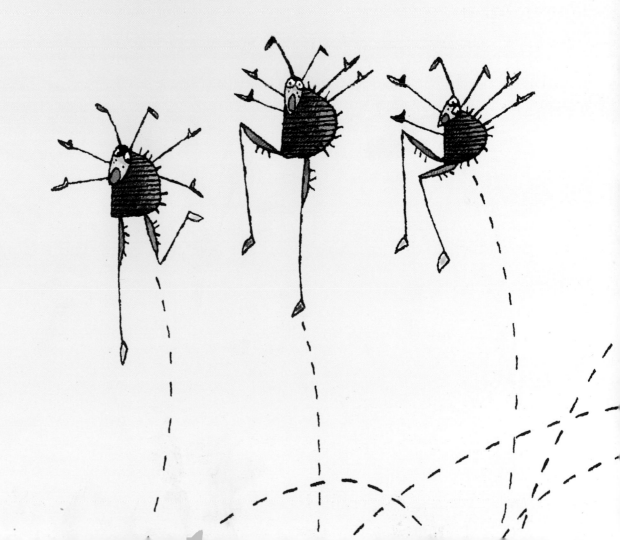

For Isobel, Gio and Jamie
U.J.

For my mum
R.A.

ORCHARD BOOKS
338 Euston Road
London NW1 3BH
Orchard Books Australia
Level 17/207 Kent Street
Sydney, NSW 2000

HB ISBN 978 1 84362 857 6
PB ISBN 978 1 40830 072 5

First published in 2008
by Orchard Books
First published in
paperback in 2009
Text © Ursula Jones 2008
Illustrations © Russell Ayto 2008

10 9 8 7 6 5 4 3 2 1

Printed in China

Orchard Books is a division of Hachette Children's Books,
an Hachette UK company.
www.hachette.co.uk

The Witch's Children Go to School

Written by
Ursula Jones

Illustrated by
Russell Ayto

ORCHARD BOOKS

One dark winter's morning, the witch's children walked past the school.

"Look out!" said the school cat.
"Here come the witch's children
and that means TROUBLE."
And it climbed onto the roof.

Gemma was outside the school gates.
"I'm going to school," she said. "It's my first day."
"We'll come too," said the eldest of the witch's children,
and they all trooped into the playground.
"So far, no trouble," mewed the school cat.

All the school children lined up and went into school. Class Three said,

"We're the biggest! No one messes with us."

"They scare me stiff," whispered Gemma. "How will I dare go into school?"

"Like this," said the Eldest One.
And he changed Gemma . . .

into . . .

an ogre.

"Ogres aren't scared of anyone,"
he said. "In you go."
And Gemma the ogre
strode into school.

"Morning!" the ogre roared at the teacher.
"I'm an ogre." And she ate the teacher's desk.

The caretaker poked the ogre with his squeezy-mop.
"Ogres out!" he shouted.

"Fee-fi-fo-fum!"
the ogre bellowed back.

Class One screamed,

Class Two shrieked

and Class Three ran into the toilets.

It was quite a squash.

"This is no good," said the ogre. "Now everyone is scared of **me**. Change me back."

"Can't," said the Eldest One. "I haven't learned how to do that yet."

The ogre cried.

"Now we've got trouble," mewed the school cat.

And the Little One laughed.
Until a teardrop flattened her.

The head teacher
telephoned the police.

The ogre hid in Class One's
Wendy house.

Then she ate it, which
quite upset Class One.

"Pardon me,"
rumbled the ogre.
"Couldn't resist."

The police arrived. "Take her away," ordered the head teacher. The ogre cried and cried.

Everyone got very wet. "A school is no place for an ogre," said the head teacher.

"Cheer up," the Middle One said to Gemma the ogre. "Watch . . ."

And she changed Class One into twelve dancing princesses and twelve swans who were really enchanted princes.

And she changed the head teacher into an emperor.

And the caretaker and his squeezy-mop into a nightingale.

She changed Class Two into gingerbread men.

And she changed the teacher into the Mad Hatter and the school cat into Puss in Boots.

With one look, she turned the policemen into Goldilocks and the Three Bears.

And then the Middle One changed the whole school into a storybook. "Now we're all stories in a book," she said. "And that's just the right place for an ogre."

"What about us?" shouted Class Three,
pushing through the crowd.
And, in a twinkling, they were fleas.
"What story are we?" they asked.

"The Forty Fleas," replied
the Middle One.
"**Thieves!**"
Class Three shrilled.

They were hopping mad.
"It's Ali Baba and the Forty
Thieves, not *Fleas*.
Make us thieves."

But the Middle One wouldn't.
"Not playing then,"
sulked the fleas.

"Let's have a dance," laughed the twelve princesses.

"Not in these boots," moaned Puss.
"They're much too big."

So the Middle One quickly
grew him into a tiger
in boots instead.

"Cool!" purred the tiger.

Then everyone danced and the nightingale sang.

And Goldilocks played the porridge bowls.

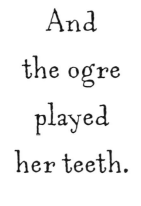

And
the ogre
played
her teeth.

And the swans did
formation flying
and the fleas held
their own disco
on one of the bears.

And they
danced and danced
UNTIL...

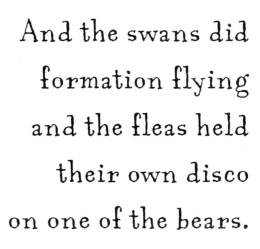

. . . the school inspector arrived.

"Disgraceful,"
hissed the inspector.
"Change this
storybook back
into a school
at once!"

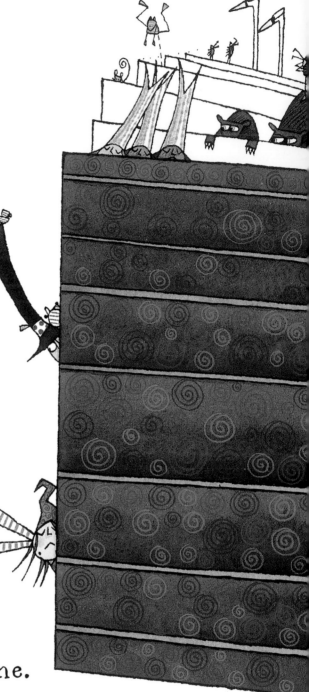

"Can't," said the Middle One.
"I haven't learned how to do that yet."

"Then I shall close the school,"
said the inspector.

"Now we're in trouble,"
trilled the nightingale.

"Now we're in trouble,"
groaned the tiger.

And the Little One laughed.
Until she sat on a flea and it bit her.

"STOP THAT!"

they all shouted.

"And get us out of trouble!"

The Little One scratched her bite.
"I don't do spells yet," she said. "I'm too little."
"Nonsense," snapped the inspector.
"You're old enough if I say so."

So the Little One made up a spell,
and the inspector turned
into a cheese – a big and
rather smelly one.

"I'm a stinker,"
wept the cheese.

"Sorry," said the Little One and tried
to turn him back.

But the cheese only grew **bigger** and
smellier. "Somebody stop me,"
he implored.

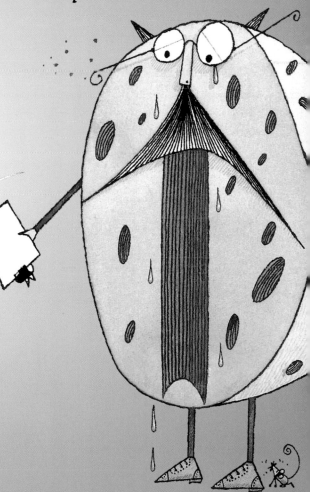

"Mum could," said the Little One.
"Then how," they all cried – gasping
for air – "can we fetch her?"

"Like this," said the Little One, and she opened her mouth wide and yelled . . .

"Socks?"

And the Eldest One shouted,
"I've lost my pants."

"I can't find my dress,"
the Middle One wailed.

And the Little One yelled,

"Where are
my socks?"

"In your
drawer,"

said a voice from the air.

And . . .

...there was
the witch on
her broomstick.
"Where
they always
are, if you
only looked,"
said the witch.

WHOOSH!

The Little One smiled.
"This is Mum," she said.
"She'll take over now."
And the witch did.

She changed the big
smelly cheese back
into the inspector.

She changed the ogre
back into Gemma.

And she changed the
storybook back into the school.

She changed all
the storybook people
back into Class One . . .

and Two . . .

and Three . . .

... and back into the caretaker and his squeezy-mop ...

and back into the teacher ...

the head teacher ...

and the policemen.

She even got the Wendy house back.

And she changed the tiger
back into the cat.

And they were all happy except the cat,
who had enjoyed being a tiger.
But the witch whispered
a secret to it and
it cheered up.

"Home time," said the head teacher.
And they all went home except the
school cat, who lived there.

The witch's children flew home
in the twilight on her broomstick.

And after tea, the witch
called to her children,

"What do you say
to cooking up
a few spells?"

"Yes," said the Eldest One.
"Please," said the
Middle One.

But the Little One
was fast asleep.

And back at the empty school, the cat became . . .

a tiger for the night, just as the witch had promised it would.